SAY HELLO, SOPHIE!

ROSEMARY WELLS

Viking

Thank you, Johanna!

VIKING
Penguin Young Readers Group
An imprint of Penguin Random House LLC
375 Hudson Street
New York, New York 10014

First published in the United States of America by Viking,
an imprint of Penguin Random House LLC, 2017

LIBRARY OF CONGRESS CATALOGING-IN-PUBLICATION DATA IS AVAILABLE

ISBN 9781101999257 (hardcover)

Manufactured in China

1   3   5   7   9   10   8   6   4   2

Set in LTC Kennerley Pro
The art for this book was created using ink, watercolor, and gouache on watercolor paper.

In the window of Belinsky's Bakery was a tray of crocodile cream puffs. Sophie wanted one.

"Hello, darlings!" said Mrs. Belinsky to Sophie and Jane.
"What do we say, Sophie?" asked Sophie's Mama.
The word **Hello** was stuck in Sophie's mouth.

Mrs. Belinsky gave Sophie a crocodile anyway.
And one for Jane.
"Ba ba!" said Jane.

The words **Thank you** wouldn't come out.
"We are going to have to practice **Big Girl Hello** and
Big Girl Thank You, Sophie," said Mama.

But it was just too embarrassing for Sophie
to say those grown-up words.

After lunch, Daddy took Jane and Sophie for a hike.
"Hello, everybody!" said the park ranger.
"Say hello, please, Sophie," said Daddy.
But Sophie couldn't say **Hello**.

The ranger gave Sophie a Junior Wolf Badge.
"What do we say, Sophie?" asked her Daddy.
Thank you shrank to the size of a pea on Sophie's tongue.
"We need to practice this **Hello** business," said Daddy.

Sophie had to practice saying **Hello** to Jane.

Sophie said **Hello** to the chickadees at the bird feeder.

Sophie said **Hello** to George Washington in the park.
"Will the **Hello** practice work?" asked Sophie's Daddy.

"I'm not holding my breath," answered Sophie's Mama.

In the library, Miss Biblio said a cheerful, "Hello, Sophie!"
"What do we say, Sophie?" whispered Sophie's Mama.
But Sophie could not quite say **Hello**.
Please and **Thank you** also vanished into thin air.

Reading behind the library encyclopedias was Granny.
Granny overheard the whole thing.

That night was Mama and Daddy's date night.
Granny was coming to babysit.

"Zeke's Palace of Ice Cream is having a sale!" said Granny.
"Let's go!" said Sophie.
"Ba ba!" said Jane. They went.

But suddenly, right outside Zeke's,
Granny said, "Oh my!
I have a toothache! I'd better sit down!
Brave girl, take charge!" said Granny.

All alone, Sophie entered Zeke's Palace of Ice Cream.
"Hello!" said Zeke.
No one was there to tell Sophie what to say.

"Hello!" said Sophie.
"Two and a half Strawberry Surprises, please!"
"Coming right up!" said Zeke.

"Thank you!" said Sophie.
"Goodbye!" said Zeke. "Come again!"
"Goodbye," said Sophie.

The Strawberry Surprise did a world of good for Granny's tooth.

Mama and Daddy came back from the movies.
"Good night, Sophie!" said Granny.
"Good night, Granny!" said Sophie.
"And good night, Jane!" said Granny.

"Hello!" said Jane.